The Cardinal & the

Crow

MICHAEL MONIZ

But they didn't. They mocked and teased him endlessly, flying
around him and calling him names all day long.

"Ugly old Crow, ugly old Crow,"

they sang.

Eventually it became too much for Crow.

He began to SQUAWK loudly at the other birds whenever they came near.

Soon, he was spending almost
all of his time alone.

The summer surrendered to fall and the leaves fell from the tree. Most of the birds flew south, following the sunshine. But Crow stayed behind, and so did Cardinal, who quite liked the cold.

Cardinal had no difficulty finding food in the chilly weather. At the edge of the forest a little feeder hung waiting for him, bursting with seed. Every morning he would swoop down for breakfast.

Crow, watching rash Cardinal from his perch
with a wary eye, decided to give some advice:

"Be careful when
fluttering around that contraption. You never
know what might be hiding somewhere below."

"**HA!** Be quiet, old Crow. What do you know? Mind your own business."

"Fine," huffed Crow. "You have been warned."

The next morning, Cardinal returned to the feeder as usual...

Suddenly a big cat leaped out from behind some bushes by the bird feeder and snatched Cardinal in his jaws.

Hearing Cardinal's screeches, Crow flew down onto a hanging branch and saw the cat was about to kill and eat his worst tormentor.

He swooped close to the feline who, as many cats like to do, was heading off to play with his prey before killing it.

"Well done, Mr. Cat," said Crow. "Only you could have caught such a quick little bird."

The vain cat pricked up his ears and paused to listen to the old crow.

"Thank you so much," Crow continued. "That cardinal has tormented me terribly. I didn't have the courage or the ability to do what you have accomplished with such ease."

The cat's eyes flashed with pride.

"Would you please, just for me, give a mighty roar?" Crow pleaded. "Only a great king of beasts, like you, can give such a roar. Let me hear and rejoice with you in your victory."

Cat was flattered. He took a deep breath,
puffed out his chest proudly and
opened his mouth wide...

Instantly, before Cat made a sound, Cardinal furiously
flapped his wings and escaped.

Cat's roar became a shrieking

MEOW

of rage.

As the two birds flew away, Cardinal turned to Crow. "Thank you. You saved me. How did you know your trick would work?"

"Because pride and foolishness often roost on the same branch," replied the wise old crow.

Cardinal opened his beak to say something clever, but when Crow turned to hear it, the little red bird grew quiet.

When spring

finally came, the singing of "ugly old Crow" was nowhere to be heard. All the birds sang happily and all were welcome on that twisted old tree, near the edge of the small forest.